AF480215

JINKY

by

H.M. Ryan

First paperback edition July 2023

Cover Illustration & Design by:
Alex Dickson

Edited by:
Hugh Barker
Scott Pack
Katherine Stephen

Special Thanks to Brendan O'Connell, Helena O'Connell, Ben Levit, Kait Richter, Katy Whitehead, Danielle Chelosky, Miranda Cundick, Gwen Montgomery, Carlos Sierra, Craig Whitney, Paul O'Connell, Jackie Squire, Tyler Donaghy

ISBN: 979-8-9870401-2-6

cosmorama

cosmoramaofficial.com

Chapter One

Sometimes Scorsese will start with a really cool shot that lets you know who the characters are and what they're like and all that. It's called an "establishing shot." He does it in *Goodfellas* and I think *Casino.* I haven't seen *Shutter Island* yet so maybe he does it in that, too. I'm sure he does. It's a trademark of his.

For this story, it's just me. If there were to be an establishing shot of my life, it would just be of me in my room.

Oh, and loads of Celtic F.C.

Celtic are the football club of the East End of Glasgow, and the one I support wholeheartedly, and will until I die. My room is a shrine to the club; my mum helped me paint the walls green-and-white stripes like the hoops on the kits.

I've put up posters of my favourite players – Larsson being my favourite, of course. Greatest non-Scotsman to ever play for the club. He was, of course, Swedish. Or *is*, rather. He's still alive.

I've also got a Kenny Dalglish poster, given to me by my grandpa, although I'm obviously too young to have seen him play. I think it's important as a supporter to have a sense of history.

Anyway, my name is Bobby, I'm 16, and I live in Springburn in Glasgow. Glasgow is in Scotland if you didn't know, and Scotland is part of the UK. There, you learned something today.

I live with my Aunt Deirdre because my mum died around this time two years ago. She had cancer. Her name was Mary and she had red hair like me. Hers was long, though, and mine is buzzed. Deirdre is her older sister and nowhere near as funny as Mum was. She's actually pretty stern. You can tell on her face. She has no lines on it. No smile lines.

My dad was some drunk named Neil – yes, like Neil Lennon – and he and my mum apparently fought like mad. I haven't seen him since I was around two because they broke up and he split for London. I don't remember any of this, though.

My nan and grandpa are still alive and I watch a ton of Celtic matches at their house. They don't live far from Deirdre and me. They're nice, though their house smells odd. Not bad, just odd. They drink loads of tea but I've started drinking coffee instead. It makes my stomach feel like shit but it's supposed to be good for you, especially in the morning.

After mum died, I went to see a psychologist. I talked to him a few times but all he did was ask how I was feeling. That's all he asked. It was a waste of time. He gave me homework, too. The bastard. He told me to write down my thoughts and feelings in a notebook whenever I was upset. I've filled out a few notebooks by now. Not because I'm upset a lot. I learned I like writing.

I have three great pals I see a lot: Mike (aka Mixer), Joe, and Thom. Mike is the leader of us, I guess since he's the oldest. He has red hair too but people don't make fun of him like they do with me. I guess that, as he's older, he knows most of those kids, so he doesn't get picked on as much. He also does a lot of the picking on me so that explains it too, I guess.

We usually hang out at parks and throw rocks at birds. Mixer and Joe have recently got into skateboards.

They're good at it. They won't let me try it.

Joe is hilarious, though. He's always making fun of me for being, in his words, "a fat ginger." It's funny because I'm not even fat, I'm just going through a growth spurt and my height hasn't caught up. I take it in stride, though. As I said, Joe's a riot.

I don't know that much about Thom. He apparently has a sister who's fit and at uni but I've never seen her.

I have a bunch of pals online as well. I used to post a lot on the BBC's 606 forum. Well, I never actually posted. I *did* spend a lot of time reading the threads on it and learning about a bunch of different stuff. A lot of the regular commenters on there were pretty funny.

BBC shut down that forum at the end of last season – which would technically be the 2010/2011 season – so someone started a Celtic-dedicated forum for all things Celtic. A few of the regular lads moved there so naturally I followed.

I love the Celtic forum because there's no drama and all that; everyone there loves Celtic, so there's no reason to fight. The only fighting comes from people talking about tactics and such, which is acceptable. Tactics are very important in football; having the right tactics ensures a positive result in a match.

The forum is also a lot less moderated than the BBC one was, which means you're free to speak your mind more than before. I often try to banter with the lads but don't often get responses.

My username is JungleBhoy. I love the song "Tarzan Boy" and I changed it from Tarzan Boy to JungleBhoy because I thought it sounded cooler and I'd never seen *Tarzan*. I added the 'h' as Celtic are also known as "The Bhoys" obviously. I've heard them called that once or twice but have read through the Celtic Wikipedia page about ten times, so I know the nickname mostly from that. As I said yesterday, it's important to have a sense of history about the club you support.

[FREE TALK]
Freebie: *its tits outside*
ElJohns1: *weather's turning early this year aye*
Freebie: *christ i'll say lol*
FKWhisperer: *earlier than last year definitely*
ElJohns1: *yeah probably not good*
6er: *global warming*
JungleBhoy: *my grandpa says global warming is a crock of shite*
6er: *uh. Its not.*
JungleBhoy: *that's just what he says. He used to work in government*
6er: *ok*

Chapter Two

My comments from last night aren't sitting well with me today.

I don't think 6er was angry at me, but it did come across a bit like I was being lectured to. I *hate* being lectured to. Even in school.

Especially in school.

I don't think I know more than the instructors. I'd have to be daft to think that. I just think I have more life experience than most of the others my age due to the amount of films I've seen. I have my own DVD player I got for Christmas a few years back and I've used it about every night since. Film is like a way to travel around the world without leaving your own bed, if you watch the films in bed like I do.

I have two subjects I like: English and Modern Studies. Modern Studies is a good mix of shit, maps and politics and shit. And English, we get to read and write a lot.

But maths and sciences. Fuck maths and sciences. I don't like when there's only one answer. That's all maths is. All of the numbers in the world and you have to find the *exact* number it is? Fuck off with that.

And sciences. I'm taking Physics and I just about want to die. The only thing I've actually learned is that gravity is -9.8, and I don't even remember what units that is.

-9.8 what? I don't fucking know.

Don't get me started about Highers. Too early to think about that, in my opinion.

At least Celtic are in full swing. Games on the weekend, slight chill in the air. What more could one ask for?

Today, I was hanging out at the park with the usual suspects –

Mixer, Joe, and Thom.

"Fat fucking chance, Mixer," Joe laughed.

"I'll prove it. Go on, give it a sniff," Mixer said, holding out two fingers at Joe. Joe swatted them away. Mixer was always doing gross stuff like that, but it was usually funny.

"There's no way you fingered Sammy Dyche during assembly, not a chance, mate," Joe pestered him. Watching those two go at it was like the Old Firm itself – though none of us supported Rangers, obviously. I just mean in terms of the enormity of the clash.

"Just because you've never done it doesn't mean I haven't," Mixer responded.

As I said, Mixer was a year older, so it made sense that he might have fingerbanged Sammy Dyche. At an assembly, though? That's vintage Mixer, to say the least.

Everyone was quiet for a few seconds. "She was so tight, too," Mixer said.

Thom shook his head. He's more of an internal thinker. He doesn't often let on what is inside his head, but you can tell there are many thoughts happening up there.

There is also a rumour that he has an absolute monster, but I haven't seen it.

"Aye, Fatboy." Mixer smacked his hand on my back then squeezed the back of my neck. "You believe me, don't ya?" Mixer called me "Fatboy" as a nickname. At first I hated it but I'd actually grown to like it.

I nodded quickly. "Yeah, 'course I do. Legendary from you, mate."

"See? Fatboy believes me. Right then, smell it, Joe."

Mixer tried to force his fingers into Joe's nostrils as Joe struggled to keep him away.

"Go on, so you can wank to it later," Mixer said.

We hung out for another hour or so – Mixer told us a story about how he had almost been arrested for graffiti when he was in Edinburgh one weekend – then I walked back to Deirdre's.

I walked in as she was making something. She was a better cook than mum. I liked eating her food.

"All right, Deirdre," I said and put my bag on the kitchen chair.

"Young Bob," Deirdre responded; it was her customary greeting for me.

"What's on the menu?" "Hungry?"

"Yeah," I said, and cracked my neck. I've been cracking it a lot lately. It feels good when I do it and feels shit when I don't.

"What'd you do after school?" Deirdre asked. She was nice but she was always wanting to know what I got up to with the boys. Sometimes it drove me up the wall.

"Nothing, was just with the boys," I answered. This usually quieted her down a bit. She smiled and nodded, then tasted some sauce with a big wooden spoon.

I had been starting to learn how to cook before mum died. Deirdre had offered to help me learn but it reminded me too much of her so we didn't.

As I've mentioned before, I love watching films. I say "films" because I have respect for the art form. Many Americans, for example, will call them "movies." I think that's shite. They're films, to me, at least.

For Christmas a few years ago, my grandparents got me a book called *1,000 Films You Must See Before You Die* and to me, that book is like the Bible, though I'm not religious.

Well.

That's a tricky subject.

I don't know if there is a God, in the sense that I grew up learning about, at least. And I know Celtic have an association with Catholicism, and I, of course, respect Jesus and the saints and that. I don't know. It's a complicated issue for me.

Anyway, I got the book alongside the DVD player.

Through the book and the films I've watched on the DVD player, I have a few favourite directors. Scorsese is definitely my favourite. The way he uses the camera to tell a story is so unique, in my opinion. His shots are all so perfect.

A second favourite director of mine is Quentin Tarantino; in my opinion, *Pulp Fiction* is one of the best movies ever made. It's pretty violent but I don't mind violent films. Violence can often add a lot to a film.

My third favourite director is George Lucas. You simply have to respect what he did with *Star Wars*. I know it's not a popular opinion on the forum, but *Revenge of the Sith* is easily my favourite of the series. *Empire Strikes Back* is a close second, though. I love the scenes on Hoth. Brilliant.

There's actually been a thread created on the forum that's all about the films that commenters have seen recently. I recently watched *Annie Hall* by Woody Allen, which was in the book, so I was eager to talk about it:

> **JungleBhoy:** *Watched Annie Hall! Great film. Comedy used to great effect. Looking forward to watching more Woody Allen :)*
> Hank: *great film.*
> R3dlaces: *he's a nonce*

I was thrilled to hear that Hank agreed with me about *Annie Hall*, but was wondering why R3dlaces would say that Woody Allen is a nonce. I looked it up and I'm still not completely certain. Something to do with cheating on his wife or something.

Anyway, my evening ritual recently has involved watching a film then going on the forum and seeing what the lads are talking about that day. There is usually some match analysis from the previous weekend's game, some transfer rumours, and a lot of taking the piss out of each other. It is so much fun watching it unfold, especially when you just *know* someone is about to get it. It is great fun. It reminds me of my mates, Mixer, Joe, and Thom.

> [FREE TALK]
> R3dlaces: *any petrolheads? need to see about my brakes, squeaking loads*
> Freebie: *laces about to be on evening news lol*
> R3dlaces: *lol trying to prevent that*
> ElJohns1: *'Local Celtic Supporter Unable to Stop Car, Wrecked by Trolley' lol*
> R3dlaces: *lol* Freebie: *lol* **JungleBhoy:** *lol*

JungleBhoy: *"A dozen dead in fiery crash, more injured" lol*
Freebie: *christ*
ElJohns1: *bit much that*

Chapter Three

My comments from last night aren't sitting well with me today, again.

In comedy, there's something called "yes, and." I've read about it on Wikipedia. I spend loads of time on Wikipedia, learning mostly about football or film, and I watched a comedy film with an improv scene in it. So I looked up what that was about and "yes, and" is a big rule in comedy.

Basically, someone says something, and you agree with it and continue with the joke. It's how jokes get funnier and funnier. I tried to do a "yes, and" with the trolley joke last night, but it seems my timing was slightly off.

I need a better plan if I am to become more of a regular on the forum. I spent most of my time at school today thinking about what to do, what to post, what to say. I respect the lads on the forum too much to waste their time with poor comments. I want to be thought-provoking. The best films are thought-provoking, anyway.

Maybe I could make fun of a player in Rangers. I could even make fun of the fact that Celtic finished second in the league the season before.

I decided to go with that, as self-deprecation is something that people seem to like. Mixer likes when I do it, for example.

I got online tonight after eating my dinner quickly, and waited for my opportunity:

> Naka87: *how we squeak by 1-0 is a disgrace*
> YokoToNeilsLennon: *mate we finished 2nd to fucking Rangers, absolute shambles*

> **JungleBhoy:** ***this coming from the club that finished 2nd to Rangers lol***
> Naka87: *there an echo in here lads? lol*
> McGonedy: *lol*
> fuckrangerscum: *fuck Rangers*

Obviously, from the "lol"s, my self-deprecation had been appreciated. However, I didn't get the exact response I wanted. I wanted it to feel like I was just bantering with lads as opposed to getting jokes in there for cheap laughs.

I moved to Free Talk, a part of the forum dedicated to what I was looking for: banter. I felt that if I could really get a foothold in there, the other users would grow to like and enjoy my banter. I even adjusted the way I typed to mirror exactly what I was seeing from the other lads:

> GlasgoFuckUrself: *lads*
> Freebie: *alright GFU, how's it*
> GlasgoFuckUrself: *mrs. made a roast. Christ. The state of it. Lol*
> Freebie: *god be with you lol*
> **JungleBhoy:** ***fuckin hate it when they make shit food. Lol***
> Freebie: *who?*
> **JungleBhoy:** ***women***
> GlasgoFuckUrself: *guess this lad hates women then? lol*

My heart dropped. I did *not* hate women. What had happened there was a bit of a panic type. I hadn't known how to answer Freebie's question and hadn't wanted it to seem like I'd only ever had nan's, Deirdre's, and mum's cooking, so I had just blurted out "women." Let me make it clear: I don't hate women and I believe in gender equality.

I was gonna try again, but I figured I'd just see what the other lads were saying. There was some really funny stuff tonight, I must say.

[POST-MATCH REACTION]
Freebie: *christ, squeaked that one out didnt we*
GlasgoFuckUrself: *must say, would rather a squeaker like this than last week's goalfest*
Naka87: *ill take the goalfest. Week's boring enough without my football being boring too*
GlasgoFuckUrself: *true enough but at least we won this week. drew last week*
Naka87: *fair*

Chapter Four

Today after school, I hung out with the boys again. Mixer and Joe held me down and made me eat bark from a tree. It was hilarious, though I did find it much funnier after I had rinsed my mouth out when I got back to Deirdre's.

[MOVIE TALK]
Freebie: *watched Inception again. Seen it lots by now but still a cracker*
GlasgoFuckUrself: *cracker indeed. Excited to see what he comes out with next*
JungleBhoy: *im a big fan of Memento myself*
GlasgoFuckUrself: *never seen it*
JungleBhoy: *also Christopher Nolan*
GlasgoFuckUrself: *yeah figured*

Chapter Five

I'm pleased with last night's performance on the forum, I must say.

I had a feeling my breakthrough would come through Movie Talk, and though I wouldn't say I've completely broken through, I feel good about my place in the forum. If I became something of a film expert, I could really establish myself on the site.

I could maybe even get that section changed from Movie Talk to Film Discussion, as it should be. I watched *The Aviator* – another Scorsese – and immediately went to post on the forum:

> **JungleBhoy:** *anyone seen The Aviator?*
> Freebie: *no*

I'm waiting for more comments to come in, but none have yet. Will report back tomorrow.

Chapter Six

No one else commented so feel like shite. Will write more tomorrow.

[MOVIE TALK]
Freebie: *just seen Moneyball. Good flick but reminded me of a few cheapie owners in the Prem lol*
GlasgoFuckUrself: *anyone specific come to mind?*
Freebie: *plenty! Some cheapskate owners for sure*
GlasgoFuckUrself: *they end up actually winning in that movie?*
Freebie: *nope lol*
GlasgoFuckUrself: *so just like the rest of the league then lol*
Freebie: *lol*

Chapter Seven

I thought about this exchange between Freebie and GFU all day today.

I slept in as it's Saturday and spent an hour or maybe more staring at the ceiling. I do this often so I can think clearer.

What came to my mind was crystal clear. Freebie and GFU were clearly friends. Their banter showed that they had known each other for a while, and were comfortable going off each other for the next part of a joke or observation.

They were "yes, and"ing each other. I need someone to "yes, and" with.

The way two great strikers can play off each other, setting each other up for goals. That's what I need on the forum.

Freebie seems to be a fun one to banter with, so I figured I'd look out for his comments and try to build off them:

[FREE TALK]
6er: *anyone fancy a 5-a-side tomorrow morn*
Freebie: *sure, long as I'm not on your team again 6er lol*
6er: *lol*
JungleBhoy: *lol yeah 6er you're fucking dogshite lol*
6er: *?*
Freebie: *ease off @JungleBhoy*

Chapter Eight

I failed once again last night.

In my attempt to jump onto Freebie's comment, I'd come across as a bit aggressive. It truly seems that I'm incapable of connecting with the lads on the forum as well as I'd like.

I get the sense that they know that I'm younger than they are, that I'm some kind of pushover. If I could just get someone to treat me like an adult, I could establish myself as a solid presence on the site.

But again, I need that striking partner. Maybe I'll make one.

Chapter Nine

Today, my maths teacher brought up Highers and I nearly shit myself.

Enough about that, though. I was thinking about my idea from last night all day today. If I created a second user on the forum, without anyone knowing it was me, I'd have flawless banter. Who better to bounce off and "yes, and" with than myself?

I was beyond excited to get home and set up a second account. I decided that, in order to get in with the lads on the forum right away, I'd need to separate myself from the others.

I decided that this second user would be someone older. I'd seen playful jokes between older and younger users before on various forums, and figured it could help set apart this account from my normal one.

As a Celtic supporter, I'd heard tons about plenty of older players from the '70s and '80s, even the '60s. I figured a good way of establishing my elder status on the forum would be naming myself after an older player. A quick Wikipedia search helped me find the perfect one: Jimmy Johnstone a.k.a. 'Jinky.' Played for Celtic from 1962 to 1975. Perfect. 'Jinky' would do, similar to 'Freebie' and a few others.

I created the second user and named him 'Jinky.' By default, the picture for new profiles was some sort of gray figure in a box. I changed it to an old black-and-white photo of Jinky.

I decided to start off with a post – as Jinky – in the Introductions thread. I thought long and hard about this; it was important to establish my knowledge of the club while making it clear that, despite the fact that I was older, I could hang with the lads:

Alright, lads.

My name isn't really Jinky – obviously that's a title that belongs to my favourite player ever to wear the green and white hoops, Jimmy Johnstone. But for now, Jinky will do just fine.

Might be a bit older than some of you so I've seen a lot of football in my life and one thing remains the same: my love for this club.

Anyway, I'm happy to talk to you lads about the club and the sport, and look forward to getting to know you all better.

Yours, "Jinky"

I read and re-read Jinky's introduction at least a dozen times before finally hitting the "Post" button. I kept refreshing the page, hoping for someone to comment on Jinky's post.

It only took about five minutes for the first response:

GlasgoFuckYourself: *cheers mate, looking forward to your insight! And welcome!*

It took about five more minutes for the next response: YokoToNeilsLennon: *cheers Jinky good to have you!* Freebie: *cheers welcome mate*

I'd never gotten this type of response on the forum before. It felt great. I figured I'd keep it going.

> Jinky: *Cheers, lads, for the warm welcome. If only the mrs'*
> *roast was as warm when it gets put on me plate. Haha!*
> Freebie: *lol*
> GlasgoFuckUrself: *I can relate! lol*

I didn't want to push things too far too quick so I said my goodnights around eleven in the evening.

Chapter Ten

This past week was all about Jinky.

The morning after my last writing, I checked the forum and saw even more responses to Jinky's introduction. Warm welcomes all around.

I was on cloud nine all week. I'd finally made friends with the lads on the board and I couldn't be happier. Now all I have to do is think of a way to make Jinky's friends *my* friends. But that will come with time.

For now, it's about learning what the lads liked to talk about. I've learned a lot just from spending time on the forum but actually talking with them will help speed up the learning process quite a bit.

I used the nights to start dropping hints that JungleBhoy and Jinky were relatives, but made sure from their typing styles that they were distinct from each other:

> [MOVIE TALK]
> Freebie: *any recommendations tonight fellas?*
> 6er: *genre?*
> Freebie: *don't care long as there's explosions I'm happy lol*
> **JungleBhoy: *the Kill Bill movies are great fun, very violent***
> **Jinky: *I second that.***

And we were off.

Deirdre sometimes knocks on the door. She probably thinks I've been using the computer for internet porn, but I have no interest in internet porn. Once Joe showed us a video of two birds kissing but that's it. No room for it when I have Celtic and film.

Chapter Eleven

I watched today's Celtic game at my grandparents' house. My home kit from last year doesn't fit anymore – a result of my growth spurt – so I just wore my Celtic jumper.

I love my grandparents but they can be a bit nosy at times.

"Any gals in your life, Bob?" my grandpa always asks with some kind of wink or smile. It makes sense. He met my nan when he was about my age; back then, lads would get married the next year or so after meeting someone.

I've got no time for a girlfriend at this point in my life. Same reason as not having the time for internet porn. I have too many other interests right now to focus on.

I do imagine what the perfect girlfriend would be like, though. It's one of those things you imagine when you are lying in bed and can't go to sleep. For me, hair colour doesn't matter. I like blondes but I also like girls with darker hair. I guess I'm flexible.

Many guys my age might like a knockout, but for me interests are more important than looks. I know I'm no stunner, for example. But I have knowledge about a lot of things and I'd be a very loyal boyfriend.

She would have to love film, of course. Not necessarily the same directors as me – though it would obviously make things easier and give us plenty to talk about right away.

One of the reasons I tend to keep my room clean is just in case a girl ever comes over. My dream is for us to watch a film then talk about what we liked and didn't like about it. Then I'd walk her home because there's no way Deirdre would let her stay over ours.

Eventually, if we fell in love and had a genuine connection, that'd be great. It'd be nice to have that part of my life figured out so I could focus on the other passions in my life.

Anyway, I said, "No," to my grandpa.

My nan sneaks me biscuits and other snacks during the game. Or at half-time, she'll say she needs help in the kitchen and ask me to come with her then she'd have a pie or some other kind of dessert there, freshly made the night before. Deirdre wouldn't like me eating it but nan is a great baker.

After the game, Deirdre and I walked back to our flat. There was a man outside the building doors, leaning against the wall, smoking a cigarette. When he saw us approach, he threw it on the cement and put it out by squishing it with his shoe. He was dressed pretty sharply.

All of a sudden, I felt Deirdre put her hand on my shoulder and push me behind her.

"Get behind me, Bobby," she whispered.

"Deirdre, what…" I started saying, but she shushed me. "Just stay behind me," she said.

The man put his hands in his pockets and shook his head as we walked towards the door.

"Dee, do we have to fuckin' make a scene of this?" he said.

Deirdre dragged me to the door past the man, who just watched us. She put her key in the door and basically pushed me inside before yelling and pointing at the lobby lift.

"Upstairs, Bobby! Upstairs now!" she shouted.

"Dee, please," the man said. She closed the door behind me.

"Shut up!" Deirdre lifted a finger at him. I watched through the glass door. "Upstairs!" she shouted one last time. I pressed the lift button – which I know she saw – then I quickly jumped behind a corner. I peeked around it so I could listen.

I could hear what they were saying. The glass was pretty thin.

"Who the fuck do you think you are?" Deirdre shouted at the man, who put his hands up.

"Dee, I know you hate my fuckin' guts…"

"There's nae a strong enough word for it. And don't fucking call me 'Dee.'"

"Fine. Fine. Just let me talk to him. You can be there too, I just want..."

Fuck do I care what you want?" He nodded.

"I'm back in town."

"Oh, la-dee-fucking-da! Fucking off to London didn't pan out, eh?"

"I know... I know I fucked up. With him. With Mary."

"Don't even utter her fucking name!" she screamed and pushed him. She began fumbling for the key again, and knowing my lift cover was blown, I sprinted upstairs.

"Dee. Deirdre," were the last things I heard him say as I ran up.

When I got to our floor, I felt like my heart was gonna jump out of my chest. I bent over and put my hands on my knees. Soon, Deirdre got out of the lift. I could tell she was trying not to cry. She might've cried a little bit on the way up, actually.

She began to unlock the door.

"Sorry for yelling, Bobby. He's some creep your mum and I used to know. Don't worry about him."

She was trying to be nice, I could tell.

"I know who that is," I said. Because I did. She looked at me so I told her.

"That's my dad, right?"

Chapter Twelve

I've never thought about my dad much. I had no idea what he looked like besides an old picture I would see sometimes. No clue what he sounded like, or what he was like at all. Sometimes I'd watch an actor in a film and I'd think, "maybe he's like this." I told this to Deirdre once and she started crying. A bit dramatic.

Deirdre asked me to sit down at the kitchen table. She made two cups of tea even though it was late and I don't drink tea anymore.

"Yes. That is your dad." "Neil, right?"

"Yes, his name is Neil." I paused for a moment.

"Don't you think I should talk to him?" "No," Deirdre said quickly.

"If he's my dad…"

"He's not anything. He's a piece… he's… no good would come of it, just trust me."

I thought again for a second before I responded, but Deirdre continued.

"He's scum, Bobby. And I don't say that for any other reason than him leaving your mum."

I wasn't sure what to say. I knew she was probably right.

"Does he live here?" I asked. I knew the answer already from what I'd heard but was playing dumb. It was a trick I learned from film.

Deirdre considered for a second. She looked at me.

"No. He lives in London."

I knew this was a lie. I had no idea how to feel at this point in time. My dad was back in town. My aunt didn't want me to even talk to him.

Deirdre gave me a hug and kissed me on the head. She'd only done that once or twice before. I went off to my room and I heard her sigh as I left. I wondered when the last time she had seen him was.

I spent the next hour or so just lying in my bed, looking at my ceiling. What else could I have done? One of my two parents – the only living one – was just yards away from me. And I had just walked past him.

If Deirdre wasn't gonna let me meet my real dad, I figured I could give JungleBhoy the chance to talk to his. Now previously, I had thought about how to connect the two accounts. Were they just mates? Or were they family? I had thought about this at great lengths during school, mostly during Physics. I settled on Jinky being JungleBhoy's dad.

I went to one of Jinky's recent posts about the previous match:

> **Jinky: Surely thought we'd miss McGeady but we have a few players looking like they might be better.**

I figured that'd be a good place to introduce the idea that Jinky and JungleBhoy were related somehow:

> **JungleBhoy: better than McGeady? already? Lads this is why you don't let your dad post on a football forum lol**

I hit 'post' without thinking twice about it. I felt such a rush, like I had just threaded a nice ball through two backs in the final third. The link was on.

The lads on the forum went mad:

> 6er: *You two related??*
> McGonedy: *This is a first lol must-be*

By the end of the night, Jinky and JungleBhoy were the toast of the site.

In film, directors sometimes work with actors a lot. Scorsese and De Niro, for example. Or Tarantino and Samuel L. Jackson. This would be that. Jinky and JungleBhoy.

Chapter Thirteen

I couldn't get to sleep last night. Jinky and JungleBhoy were on my mind. I thought of situations where the two could interact, giving each other shit and passing banter back and forth. Jinky would definitely be the way to get JungleBhoy really stuck in on the forums.

I eventually did fall asleep – it must have been just short of four in the morning – and the day at school really dragged. More talk of Highers. Makes my skin crawl.

I decided not to tell Mixer and the other boys about seeing my dad. I remember the one time I had talked about my dad – not that there was much to talk about – Mixer had given me a hard time. I'm usually fine with that, but I have too much to worry about right now.

Deirdre was standing outside the flat building doors when I got home, with a blanket wrapped around her shoulders, which she squeezed tight.

"Young Bobby," she said with a smile. "Hiya, Deirdre. Why are you out here?" Deirdre's smile remained.

"Needed some air. Come on, then."

She got up and wrapped half the blanket around me even though I wasn't cold. Dinner felt normal; there was no mention of Neil or anything related to mum. I'm a little relieved, to be honest. I don't want things to change all that much, especially now that I had the forums to look forward to.

Tonight, after dinner, presented a bit of an opportunity:

[FREE TALK]
GlasgoFuckUrself: *bit heavy maybe but mrs is in the hospital. Cough that got worse so just precaution, up a wall about it still*

I considered for a moment, then started typing:

Jinky: *I've been there before, GFU. Stay strong, mate. She needs your support now more than ever.*

I thought again.

Jinky: *You'll get through this. Trust me.*

It felt nice to have Jinky's perspective despite being younger myself. It felt like I had been through it already and was ready to provide help to a friend:

GlasgoFuckUrself: *thanks Jinky mate. Maybe I'm just weepy but good to have a bloke like you around lol*
JungleBhoy: *speak for yourself, GFU. lol*
GlasgoFuckUrself: *lol*
Freebie: *lol*

Chapter Fourteen

It's Friday.

After school, I was walking back home. I wasn't meeting up with the lads today so I decided I'd go home and pop on a film. As I walked, I heard someone sort of whispering my name. I looked ahead and it was Neil.

After I saw him, he just started talking quick.

"Bobby, look. Just give me a second. I know you're probably furious with me."

I stopped and stared at him as he paused. He was probably waiting for some kind of answer. Then he kept going.

"I just want to talk to you. Explain myself, maybe." Neil put his hands in his coat pockets.

"Bobby, I'm not gonna pretend I can make it all up to you. But let me talk to you. Please."

I didn't know what to say. I didn't hate him. I felt nothing for him.

"Sure," I answered.

He smiled briefly before suggesting a café nearby.

I sat there, across the table from him. I've often passed this café but had never been inside before. He was tapping his foot and just looking at me.

"We should probably wait until we order before I sort of go into this whole thing," he said.

"I'm not hungry," I answered. He furrowed his brow. "Really?" he asked.

"What do you mean, 'really'?"

Neil put his hands up.

"That's not... I didn't mean it like that. I just... it's almost dinnertime, isn't it?"

"Well, are you gonna eat?" "No, probably not."

"Okay."

Neil nodded. The server approached.

"Water's fine, thank you," Neil said, grabbing my menu and putting it on top of his and handing it to her.

The server flicked her brows and took the menus anyway. Neil kept tapping his foot before finally speaking once the server walked away.

"I bet you have a million questions for me right now," he said.

I thought for a second.

"Not really," I responded. I had a few, of course, but not 'a million.'

He nodded. I shrugged.

"What's your surname?" I asked. "Kelly," he answered.

"Neil Kelly?" "That's right."

"What do you do for work?" "I'm an actor."

My eyes shot open. "Like in films?" I asked.

He smiled but shook his head.

"Haven't been in any films. Mostly theatre. A few commercial shoots. Nothing major."

I slumped back in the booth before nodding my head. "Theatre is cool, though. I've never seen one."

"Seen what?" "A play."

Neil furrowed his brow.

"You've never seen a performance?" "No."

"Well, we'll have to sort that out straight away!"

Neil smiled and so did I, until I remembered Deirdre.

"My aunt doesn't want us to talk so she probably wouldn't like that."

Neil shook his head and looked to the side.

"Ah, Dee is Dee. I'm your dad. It could be good for us to spend some time together."

I nodded. It could be.

"I'm not joking about the theatre, we should go!" Neil said. He seemed so excited now.

"That sounds great," I responded. "How's tomorrow? One not too far!" "Sure."

Later, Neil said he'd walk me home.

We got to the corner where I turn to head to the flat building when Neil stopped suddenly.

"Right, look," he started. "Probably shouldn't tell your aunt that you saw me today. She probably... she's probably still a bit upset."

"I won't," I responded.

"Right, then," Neil said. "And we're on for tomorrow. At the theatre?"

"Yeah, sounds good." "Good lad."

We stood there for a few seconds before he put his hands in his pockets.

"Take care, then," he said before nodding and starting to walk off.

"Bye," I said back.

When I got in, Deirdre asked where I had been and I told her I had been with Mixer and the boys. After dinner, I spent some time on the forums as Jinky and JungleBhoy.

[FREE TALK]
GlasgoFuckUrself: *lads*
JungleBhoy: *GFU, how's the mrs holding up?*
GlasgoFuckUrself: *much better, cheers JB. your da's words really helped*
JungleBhoy: *so good to hear :)*

Chapter Fifteen

It was easier to get to sleep last night than previous nights. I guess the rush of everything was starting to wear off.

Today, though, my heart was actually pounding at times, thinking about seeing a play with Neil. I don't know if I was more nervous about seeing a live performance or if it was spending more time with my dad.

Neil told me to dress nicely for the show, so I put on a shirt and jeans. Deirdre was in the kitchen, which of course I had to pass to get to the front door. She saw me through the kitchen doorway.

"Well, well, well! Where is young Bob going dressed like this?" she asked.

I hadn't thought of what to say beforehand. "I'm going to meet up with the lads for dinner."

Deirdre cocked her head, asking, "Dinner, eh? A fancy one?"

"Yeah. We have a lot to discuss, actually."

Deirdre narrowed her eyes. I'd been doing a lot of lying to Deirdre but I didn't know what else to do. I couldn't tell her I was going to meet up with Neil.

Deirdre then nodded slowly. "Right, then. Back before eleven."

"Sure, Deirdre," I responded.

"I mean it. Eleven." She pointed at me and I nodded. "Love you," I said. She smiled.

"Love you."

It wasn't a long walk to the theatre from our flat. Like the café, I'd passed the theatre hundreds of times and always wondered what a show in there would be like. It was exciting knowing I'd actually be experiencing one.

A lot of boys my age would probably not be as excited about going to the theatre, but as someone who appreciates good narrative, I was looking forward to it. Theatre is like film in many ways, only it's live as opposed to filmed.

Neil was outside, once again dressed smartly. I guess this is a signature of his. He was pacing around with his hands in his jacket pockets. He nodded as I walked towards him.

"No other trousers?" he asked. "Huh?"

"You've got jeans."

"Oh. Yeah, I thought they looked sharp." Neil nodded again. "Right then. Ready?"

We went in and took our seats. Neil told me that this was a performance of *Waiting for Godot*, which he said was by an Irish playwright named Beckett. It's about two mates who wait for this lad named Godot, and they talk the whole time.

It was very philosophical.

I could also tell that Neil was looking at me sometimes, probably to see if I was enjoying it. I *was* but I felt this pressure to smile whenever he looked at me. So I was just smiling at him periodically throughout the play. I probably looked mad.

After the show, neither of us really knew what to do. We just stood outside the theatre. Neil smoked a cigarette.

"Do you smoke?" he asked.

"Not really," I answered, which was true. I'd only had a few in my life. One time Mixer made me smoke five at once. I still feel like every time I cough it's from that.

"Good," he said, looking off and taking another drag. I nodded and put my hands in my jeans pockets.

"Oh, what are you doing next Tuesday, after school?" Neil asked.

"Nothing, I don't think."

"Want to come with me to an audition? It's for a play, actually."

"Sure, I'll go." "Great!"

Neil took another drag.

"Right then. Walk you home?"

I nodded and Neil threw down his cigarette then squished it with his foot. He walked me back to the corner, we said our goodbyes, and I went into the flat.

I feel things are going well with Neil, despite the fact that I am lying to Deirdre so much. But it feels like one of those things that we'll laugh about when we are older.

Like, "Oh, remember how cheeky I was being! Being a cheeky lad." I can picture it perfectly, Deirdre in a wheelchair with a blanket over her legs and me, tall and strong, wheeling her around the park. That thought makes me happy.

[MOVIE TALK]
ElJohns1: *anyone seen The Artist? French movie*
GlasgoFuckUrself: *the one with fuck all talking in it?*
ElJohns1: *aye thats the one*
GlasgoFuckUrself: *yeah, boring*
Jinky: *I thought it did a great job expressing emotion without dialogue. A lot of great films do that. It's a sign of great direction.*
JungleBhoy: *i agree with the old man*
Freebie: *agreed, liked it*

Chapter Sixteen

Today was dogshite, school-wise.

I have a massive maths test tomorrow that I've barely revised for. My own fault, really, but to be fair to myself I've had a lot going on lately.

I got home from school and took out my books and notebooks for maths. I revised the first few pages before truthfully, I spaced out. My mind was bouncing back and forth between the forum and Celtic and Neil and Deirdre, with sprinkles of film in there. School was firmly in the back of my mind at this point. Deirdre would be shocked to hear this. Mum, too. That's the really crushing one.

I can't help it, though. I'd wager I have more going on right now than a normal lad my age. Most people have dads that have been there the whole time. Might yell at them loads but still there. And if they've fucked off, they at least stay fucked off. Neil is back. My dad is back. I haven't a clue how to handle it.

[FREE TALK]
GlasgoFuckUrself: *how we feelin about the weekend, lads*
Freebie: *long ways to it lol* GlasgoFuckUrself: *meant the match free* Freebie: *I know lol feeling alright about it*
JungleBhoy: *im predicting a big win personally*
Freebie: *me too*
JungleBhoy: *predicting big things for Hooper, think he's about to go on a run of form*
Jinky: *I agree. Looks a tidy signing.*
Freebie: *anyone want to meet up for it?* GlasgoFuckUrself: *aye, could use a few hours out* I considered for only a

moment before typing.
JungleBhoy: *i'm in*

Chapter Seventeen

I don't know what I was thinking.

I've never been in a pub before. I have no real interest in alcohol anyway. I know it's not about the alcohol, it's about chatting with the lads, but what if they expected Jinky to be there, too? Would they be disappointed that it was just JungleBhoy?

That's a problem for the weekend.

For today, I got to see Neil do an audition.

I feel like Deirdre is getting suspicious but what can she do? It's my decision to hang with my dad. She just has to deal with it, I suppose.

I met Neil outside the building where he was going to audition, a smaller theatre in Glasgow. He seemed a bit fidgety.

"Right, then," he started as he began to pace. "This is a play about a man called Martin, a businessman who has to sell something very precious to him: his own heart."

I had no idea what he meant by this.

"You see, Martin is dying of a rare disease that eats away at his bones, yeah? But his heart is perfectly fine. So he has to use his skills as a salesman to sell his heart to the highest bidder in the hopes of raising some money for his family before he dies from the bone disease."

"Sounds like a drama," I said. Neil nodded.

"It's a drama. I'm gonna audition for Martin."

Neil took another drag from his cigarette.

"Martin's what's called a 'juicy part.' Those are the parts you wanna play."

I nodded.

"A juicy part. That's a good term. De Niro has a lot of those."

Neil nodded again. "He does."

Neil threw the cigarette down on the ground and squished it with his foot.

"Right, then. Ready to go in?"

I nodded and he nodded back, then took a deep breath. It was much less glamorous than the theatre we saw the play in, but it at least had a stage and everything. I sat near the back of the theatre while Neil said he had to go backstage and sign in.

I watched as actor after actor auditioned. The actors all seemed good; they were delivering the lines with real pain, which I would be looking for if I were the director. It would be tough for me to choose just one actor, really.

Then it was Neil's turn. He walked on stage and clasped his hands together.

"My name is Neil Kelly, and I'm auditioning for the role of Martin."

The director said something I couldn't hear then Neil took a breath.

"I'm here. Or at least, I'm here if you need me," Neil began. He looked a certain way. Maybe 'vulnerable' would be the word. The same way he's looked when talking to Deirdre.

One of the people in the front row of the theatre – I'm guessing one of the directors – began to respond, reading from a script, I guessed. There was no real emotion in her voice.

"Martin, you know you don't have much time left," she began. "What makes you think you can sell your heart before you die of the rare bone disease? Is that even legal?"

Neil looked down, shook his head, then looked back up.

"I have to. I have to leave you and little Tommy in a better position when I'm gone. Even if it takes selling my heart, which has been untouched by the rare bone disease and is perfectly healthy."

I could definitely see someone like Spielberg directing this in a film. It was chock full of emotion.

"Little Tommy and I will be fine, Martin. You need to rest. Lugging around that big suitcase is only going to hurt your bones more," the director answered.

Neil closed his eyes.

"My bones may crumble to dust, but my love for you will never fade."

"Oh, Martin," the woman said lifelessly. "I'll always love you, too. Now kiss me."

Neil smiled, and then pretended that he was holding a woman's face and kissing it. It looked *convincing*. It was almost like he *was* kissing an invisible woman.

I believed him.

There were a few seconds of silence. Neil smiled and put his hands around his back. I think the directors were whispering with each other.

"Thank you very much, Mr. Kelly. We'll be in touch," one of the directors finally said.

Neil bowed and clapped his hands together.

"Thank you, ladies and gentlemen. I appreciate your time," he said before walking off the stage.

I watched as another man started to audition the same scene, then Neil tapped me on the shoulder.

"Ready to go?" he whispered.

"I'm watching this guy audition," I answered. Neil lowered his brow.

"This guy's shit. Come on," he whispered back. I got up and followed him out into the lobby and then outside.

"What'd you think?" Neil asked.

"You were great," I said. I really meant it, too. I thought he had shown a lot of intensity and emotion.

"Thanks, Bobby," Neil said, smiling. "I felt a little stiff but I think my performance came through towards the end."

"Yeah, I agree," I responded.

Neil seemed happy. The first few times I'd seen him, he'd always seemed nervous.

It felt like a good time to ask him something I had started to wonder about.

"Did you love my mum?" I asked.

Neil looked at me and stopped walking, his hands in his coat pockets. I could see his breath.

"What?" he answered.

"When I was born. Did you love each other?" Neil looked off for a second.

"Course I did," he almost whispered.

I smiled. Again, I believed him. We must not have been paying attention, though, as we rounded the corner together. The one right before my building.

"You piece of shite!" I heard. The voice was very familiar; it was Deirdre's.

"Oh, Christ," Neil whispered.

Deirdre approached from behind, clutching her coat with her arms tightly crossed.

"I tell you to fuck off so what do you do? Sneak around with the son you don't give a shit about?" she shouted.

"What do you know about how I feel about my own son, Dee?" Neil snapped back.

"If I see you in the same fucking *neighbourhood* as Bobby again, I'm getting the police involved," Deirdre warned.

"Deirdre, it's okay, I'm..." I started.

"You better not say a word, Bobby. You're in deep shit as it is."

I immediately stopped talking. Deirdre pointed at Neil. "I mean it. I'll get a court order."

Neil looked down and shook his head.

"Dee, please."

Deirdre grabbed my arm and started to back away. "Fuck off, Neil."

Deirdre led me by the arm all the way home.

Oh, and I should also mention: I fucking bombed that maths exam.

> [FREE TALK]
> **Jinky:** *A word of advice, lads. In life, honesty is always the best policy. Otherwise, it leads to trouble. Just a tip from your older pal, Jinky.*

Chapter Eighteen

Excuse my language, but I'm fucked.

Deirdre caught me hanging out with Neil, which she had expressly told me *not* to do. She's watching me like a hawk whenever I walk around the flat. I've also caught her looking out the window at the pavement a few floors down a couple times. Neil hasn't given me his phone number so there's no way for me to reach him, anyway.

I've never really been punished before, so it's an interesting experience. I can still watch films and Celtic, so all isn't lost. Deirdre did set a curfew of 6:30 for me on schooldays, though.

I was hanging with the lads at the park. It had been a bit since I'd seen them and obviously they'd been talking about it.

"Where've you been, mate?" Mixer asked.

I didn't know how to answer. But I liked Mixer so I tried. "Actually, have been with my dad."

"Your dad? The one who fucked off?" Mixer asked, smiling at Joe.

"Yeah. Not gonna see him for a while now, though," I answered. Joe laughed.

"Fucked off again, did he? Can't say I blame him."

"What'd you say?" I asked. I didn't really think about saying that, I just sort of did.

Mixer turned to Joe and laughed.

"Come on, Fatboy. You wouldn't exactly be anyone's pride and joy," he said. "No disrespect."

My blood went hot. That's the only way I can describe it. I could feel my teeth clenching. This wasn't something I'd felt in a while, maybe ever. Not much made me angry. But this was doing it.

"Fuck off, mate," I said as Mixer and Joe laughed. Thom sat there as usual. I had had enough and started walking from the half-wall they were all sitting on.

"Aye, maybe you'll find your dad on the way home, Fatboy!" Joe yelled out to me.

"Nah, he's probably busy wanking to old pictures of your mum," Mixer yelled after.

I turned around and walked fast towards them. They were laughing. As hard as I could, I pushed Mixer off the half-wall. He fell with a slam onto the grass behind the wall. I tried to push Joe too, but he gripped the wall and kicked me away.

"Fuck are you doing?" Joe yelled. He hopped off the wall and pushed me. I tripped over my feet and fell on my arse. As I got to my feet, I turned only to feel a fist smashing into my nose.

The pain was sharp and my eyes filled with water. I felt someone kneel next to me, then another punch, this time to my mouth. It was Mixer. I could tell from his voice.

"Nutted up, have you, Fatty?" he said.

After the second punch, he got up. I got kicked in the stomach. I lost my breath and couldn't catch it. I was on my side, and blood poured from my nose down my cheek and onto the grass.

I got kicked again in the chest.

"Come on, mate, let's go!" one of them said. I heard the three of them run away, laughing as they did. I tried to wipe my eyes but ended up wiping blood from my nose into them. I eventually caught my breath and rolled over onto my stomach. I was alone in the park.

There was no hiding it from Deirdre. I tried to hustle past her to go to the bathroom but she saw me pass from the main room. She got up and came after me; before I could close the bathroom door, she held it open and put a hand to her mouth.

"Bobby, Christ, what happened? What the hell happened?"

I turned on the tap as Deirdre grabbed a towel from the cupboard.

"Look at me," she ordered and started wetting the towel in the sink. "What happened? Who did this?"

"Nobody. I tripped."

"You tripped? Christ, Bobby, did you trip five times? Who did this?"

"Nobody, I'm telling you."

Deirdre started patting at my face, which really stung. I winced in pain. I couldn't tell her who had done this.

Mixer, Joe, and Thom were my best mates. I couldn't go telling Auntie Deirdre just because they punched and kicked me just a bit.

"Bobby," Deirdre whispered. She put her hands on either cheek.

I decided I'd tell her a partial truth. "These older lads, at the park." Deirdre shook her head.

"And why?"

I looked off to the side.

"They said something about mum. So I..."

I suddenly got the urge to cry, which I'd only done at *E.T.* before, during the scene where they're experimenting on E.T. That always makes me cry. But then suddenly I was crying and Deirdre was holding me. I didn't know how it started until I was already doing it.

Deirdre put some kind of cream on the cuts, then told me to shower. When I got out, she had fetched me a glass of water and we watched a film together in the main room.

Chapter Nineteen

Went to the doctor and it was shite. He kept touching my nose and it hurt like hell. I have to bandage it and keep changing the bandage.

And I still had homework to do even though I didn't go to school.

Shite day.

Chapter Twenty

Deirdre let me stay home from school today, telling them I was sick. Which was good because we probably got our maths exams back. I always hate that. Teacher walking around with the exams in hand, passing them out, giving smiles or stern looks, depending on the grade. Awful experience. Has to be a better way to do that.

Deirdre had to go to work so I spent all day watching films. I took a nap later in the afternoon in my bed.

I woke up and heard a conversation in the main room. I walked in to see Deirdre and Neil. They both said hello to me at the same time.

"Have a sit, Bobby," Deirdre said, in her typical low voice. Neil had a half smile, and his hands were folded. I could tell he was inspecting my cuts and bruises on my face.

I sat down between Deirdre, who was in the armchair, and Neil, who was on the other end of the sofa. Deirdre started.

"So, I know just about every interaction you've seen between me and... your father... hasn't been pleasant."

I looked at Neil who shrugged then nodded. Deirdre continued.

"But that's because we have a... we have a bit of a history."

Deirdre nodded at Neil, who cleared his throat.

"Right. A lot was said when I... a lot was said when I left. Things I regret. Certainly."

His voice trailed off before he straightened up in his seat.

"There's a lot I need to make right. And I'm grateful... I am, Dee... I'm grateful that your aunt is giving me the chance to do so."

I lowered my brow, which hurt my face.

"Is this because I got beat up at the park?" I asked.

Deirdre and Neil shook their heads vigorously and both said some variation on "no." Deirdre got up and sat down on the arm of the sofa, putting her arm around me.

"I think it's important... and this took a lot of thinking, I'll be honest... but I think it's important for you to have some kind of relationship with your father. Even if it's under *intense* supervision..."

Deirdre paused and looked at Neil who nodded. "...So we're gonna give Neil that chance."

I looked at the ground.

"If you want to, that is," she continued. I looked at Deirdre.

"Sure."

Neil jerked back in his seat before recovering and clasping his hands back together.

"Great, that's... that's wonderful, Bobby." Deirdre nodded and leaned forward.

"Now, it's important to say: if you ever feel uncomfortable with Neil, you tell me right away, yeah?"

I nodded. Neil looked at Deirdre as he started to talk.

"Right. That's important. But I won't be doing anything to make you feel that way. I promise."

Deirdre returned Neil's look.

"But if he does, you just tell me straight away."

Neil nodded and opened his mouth, then closed it again. "Right," he finally said.

We all sat there for a few moments. "Bobby, you up for a walk?" Neil asked. I shrugged.

"Sure. Not doing anything." "Right, then. Let's hit it."

Deirdre got up and squeezed my shoulder before leaning against the doorframe. She locked eyes with Neil as he walked by her, and he nodded to her.

We walked out of the building and Neil gave me a pat on the back.

"Forgot to tell ya, mate. Didn't get that part I auditioned for."

"Ahh. I'm sorry." Neil shook his head.

"S'alright. You gotta get used to rejection when you're an actor. When you're an artist, really."

I agreed with him. Lots of actors and directors go through this sort of thing. It comes with the territory.

I suddenly had an idea, and before I could think it through, I was talking.

"I'm meeting up with some lads from a Celtic forum I post on Saturday and I..."

"You're what?"

"I'm meeting up with some lads from..."

"No, I heard you, but who are these 'lads from a Celtic forum'?"

"Oh," I said. "Well, there's Freebie, and ElJohns1, and of course GlasgoFuckUrself..."

Neil stopped in place. "Pardon?"

I stopped too.

"Oh, it's just his username. Pretty cheeky, eh?"

"That's not a good idea, mate. You're a teenager, you should not be meeting people from the internet."

"Well, I thought you'd say that, which is why I had an idea. Why don't you come? I could say you're my uncle."

"Why not just say I'm your da?"

"Because my da is Jinky."

Neil squinted. "What?"

"Right, then," I said. Christ, I was starting to sound like Neil. "I wasn't getting on with the lads on the forum, and felt I needed a 'striking partner', someone to banter with. So I made a second account on there and said he was my da."

"Why?"

"So I could banter with him easier, and then banter with the other lads. In any case, me and Jinky..."

"Who's Jinky?"

"My da!"

"I'm your da!" Neil said with, throwing his hands up.

"I know! But not on the forum! It's Jinky on the forum."

Neil shook his head. I could see the gears turning in his head.

"Anyway," I continued. "They're meeting up on Saturday for the Celtic game at a pub and it might be good if you came along. I trust these lads, they're my mates now, but could be fun."

Neil sighed.

"And I can't just say I'm your da? I have to say I'm some uncle?"

"Jinky is older..."

"Who's Jinky, again? Jimmy Johnstone?" "Yes, but also my da."

Neil looked at me blankly.

"On the forum," I continued. "That's his username." "Right."

"But they know Jinky as an older bloke, older than you. So it wouldn't match up."

Neil looked off past me. "Right."

"So you can be Uncle Neil, yeah?" Neil sighed again before nodding.

"Sure, mate. I'll be Uncle Neil. Not letting you go to this pub by yourself."

"Great, thanks, Neil."

I was excited. It'd be like worlds colliding. My dad – as my uncle – would be meeting my mates from online. Thrilled!

We walked some more in a sort of loop before returning back to the flat. We agreed to meet there on Saturday morning for the walk to the pub to meet the lads from the forum.

JungleBhoy: *looking forward to seeing you lads on Saturday!*
Freebie: *same here JB!*
GlasgoFuckUrself: *will be great!*

Chapter Twenty-One

Guess I'll dive right into it. No sense in beating around the bush.

Neil met me outside the building in the morning. He winced when he saw my bandaged nose. He was wearing a Celtic scarf. It looked class. I wore my usual Celtic jumper.

The pub wasn't far away, maybe fifteen or so minutes. On the way, I filled Neil in on all of the banter between the lads: Freebie was a nice bloke, GFU had a bit of an edge to him, and ElJohns1 was a bit of a mystery.

We got to the pub and there were a few people in Celtic colours around the place. I saw three lads at the counter itself, looking at me and Neil and whispering. One walked up to us.

"You lads JB and Jinky?" I smiled.

"I'm JB. Jinky's, um… a bit under the weather, unfortunately."

"Ah, that's too bad," the man said. He was bald with a beard.

"This is my uncle Neil, though."

"How's it, Neil?" the man said, reaching out to shake his hand. "I'm Fred, known as Freebie on our wee forum.

Come on, come meet the other lads."

Fred walked back towards the others. Neil leaned in towards me.

"JB?"

"JungleBhoy. My username," I responded before following Fred over to his mates.

"Lads," Fred started. "This is GFU, or Geoff."

Fred motioned to the man with the moustache, who nodded and smiled at us.

"All right, JB," Geoff said.

"You can call me Bobby. This is my uncle Neil." "All right, Bobby. All right, Neil."

Fred then pointed at the third man.

"And this here's Sam, or ElJohns as you probably know him."

"Cheers, lads. Good to meet you," Sam said. "Get you something to drink?" Fred asked Neil.

"I'm okay, cheers," Neil answered. I remember being told once years ago that Neil was a drunk. I guess he wasn't anymore.

"What happened to your face, Bobby?" Sam asked. I had nearly forgotten about my nose.

"I, erm… got in a bit of a fight after school," I answered. It felt nice telling the truth for a change. I felt a bit bad lying to them about Neil, like I felt bad about lying to Dee before. It seemed like no matter what recently, I was always lying to someone. It didn't sit right with me. So it was nice to tell the truth, even if it was a little thing.

"Been there, back in the day," Geoff said with a laugh. "Did you at least get a few shots of your own in?"

"Need backup, mate, we're there," Sam said, putting his fists up. I smiled.

"So you lads are on this website, then?" Neil asked, his hands still in his coat pockets.

"Yeah, mate. Moved over to this new one from the old BBC one that got shut down," Geoff said. "JB and his da have become some regulars on there, I'd say."

"I'd have to agree," Sam said with a smile. "Is that right?" Neil said, raising his brow. "That your brother then?" Geoff asked Neil. "Who?" Neil answered.

"Jinky. That your brother?"

Neil bit his bottom lip briefly before looking at me.

"Yeah. Yeah, Jinky's my brother. Bit sick right now, though. Yeah."

"Hope it's not too serious," Fred said, and shook his head.

"Should be fine. Should bounce right back," Neil said with a nod.

"He's great fun," Geoff nodded. "Really helped me out recently. Not sure if Bobby told you, about my wife and all. She's actually been sick recently herself."

"Sorry to hear that." Neil took his hands out of his pocket and began to play with the cuff of one of his sleeves.

"She's better now, though. Thankfully. But Jinky's words really stuck with me. Something so simple yet so... it really helped," Geoff continued.

I looked up at Neil, who was already looking at me.

"That's him," Neil said with a smile. "Always looking to help."

We watched the rest of the game with the lads from the forum and hung out for a bit afterwards as well. They were great fun.

We left the pub and started our walk home. Neil stopped in front of a store on the way and looked up at the sign. It was a bicycle store.

"Why've we stopped?" I asked. Neil furrowed his brow at me.

"Worth a look," he responded before smiling. He pushed the door open and walked in.

I stood there for a few moments looking through the glass door. Neil started talking to the shopkeeper before waving me in. I opened the door, which caused the bell at the top to ring.

"...will need a bigger one," Neil finished saying. I looked around at all of the bikes on the walls and hanging from the ceiling. I didn't know anything about bikes and hadn't ridden one in years.

"What would you recommend for my son here?" Neil asked the shopkeeper.

I looked at Neil, or at least at the back of his head. I don't think I had heard him call me that so directly before.

The shopkeeper showed us a bicycle, Neil looked at me, I nodded, Neil paid, and we walked out of the bicycle store. I now have a bicycle.

I pushed the bicycle with Neil walking next to me.

"Thank you again, Neil. This is really nice of you," I told him.

"Every kid needs a bike," he said.

We came to the road that goes past the park and I prayed to God that the boys wouldn't be there, even though, again, I'm not religious. As we got closer and walked by the park, though, I saw them in their usual spot. They had their skateboards and were trying to do tricks on the pavement.

I immediately looked away, which Neil, I guess, noticed. "What is it?" he asked.

"Nothing," I said as I began to walk with the bicycle faster.

"What's the matter?" he asked again. "Nothing, let's just hurry."

I glanced again at the boys and Neil followed my eyes. He stopped in place as I kept walking.

"That them?"

I looked over my shoulder. "That who?"

Neil took his hands out of his pockets. "That's them, isn't it?" he said lowly.

I shook my head as I walked.

"Right, then," he said and began to walk on the grass towards them. I stopped walking and dropped the bike.

"Neil, stop! They're my mates!" I said, trying to get him to turn around. I couldn't shout because I'd get their attention. So I sort of whisper-shouted.

It didn't work. Neil continued walking on the grass in their direction.

"Shit! Shit!" I whispered and took cover behind the trash bin nearby. I peeked around the edge of it. I heard Neil shout at the boys.

"Alright, boys. How's it?"

"What's up, geezer?" Mixer answered.

Neil laughed. "Geezer! That's funny. You're funny, mate." The boys looked at each other.

"See you've got some boards with you," Neil continued. "I used to skate back in the day myself."

"Back in the fifties?" Joe responded, and the boys laughed. Neil smiled.

"Fifties. 'Cause I'm old. Nice one. Mind if I give it a go, then? If you don't mind a geezer showing you up, that is."

Mixer and Joe looked at each other. Mixer handed Neil his skateboard, stickers covering the underside.

"Thanks, *mate*," Neil said, grabbing the board. I watched and thought about running over, but I didn't want to reveal myself.

Neil walked towards the pavement near the half-wall. He placed the skateboard on the cement.

"See, back when I grew up…" he placed a foot on the board, "…there were checks and balances."

The boys turned around to face Neil on the pavement.

"And if you fucked with someone…" Neil stepped and began to row with his foot, "…you could be sure that you'd get fucked with back."

The boys kept on watching. I saw Joe and Mixer look at each other. Neil put his other foot on the board and effortlessly skated away from them. He crouched lower and turned with the board, heading back towards the boys on the half-wall.

He skated a few more yards before skidding to a stop and flipping one end of the board into his hand.

"So let's just get this straight: you fuck with anyone again. Anyone. And I'll beat the fuck out of you."

Neil dropped the end of the skateboard onto the cement, stepped back, lifted his foot, and stomped on it, right in the middle. The board snapped cleanly in half.

"What the fuck, mate?" Mixer and Joe jumped off the wall as Thom's jaw dropped. Neil dropped his suit jacket to his elbows and stared them down.

"I fuckin' mean it," he said. Almost growled.

Joe and Mixer stepped forward but stopped a good distance away from Neil. Joe and Mixer stared before Joe tapped Mixer on the back.

"Come on, mate," he whispered.

"Fuck off, geezer! Psycho shit, that!" Mixer shouted, backing away. Thom hopped off the wall and followed the two as they began to walk quickly away from Neil. Even he looked shocked.

Neil flicked his jacket back above his shoulders. I couldn't believe what I had seen. I grabbed my bike and began to jog forward before hopping on. I didn't see Neil as I sped off back home.

I threw the bike against the building wall and opened the door before making my way to our flat.

I slammed my bedroom door and started pacing around the

room. I held back tears as I ran my hands over my head. Don't
know why I was close to crying but I was. I tried to calm myself
down by sitting in my desk chair. I had left the forums open.

I was on JungleBhoy. I clicked and created a new thread on the
forums: "SERIOUS: some life news..."

Before I knew what I was really doing, I began to type:

> Many of you on this forum have grown to like and
> appreciate my father – Jinky – and his stories and
> thoughts about Celtic.
> It is with great sadness that I now tell you that Jinky has
> passed on. It was sudden and unexpected.
> I'm sorry to share this news.

Without a second thought, I posted the thread.

Chapter Twenty-Two

I woke up to a lot of messages. A lot.

The lads on the forum had flooded the thread I had started the night before.

There were so many offers of support.

My heart dropped. I had meant Jinky to be a sort of starting point for my own presence on the forum: someone to banter with as I got to know the lads better. I hadn't meant to ever kill Jinky. I thought he would just ride off into the sunset at some point, leaving the younger lads to have their fun.

I had no idea what to do. People wanted to do charity runs in Jinky's name. He had become a pillar of this Celtic forum. And now I'd killed him.

Then, people started to ask about funeral services. Funeral services? What the fuck would I bury?

I couldn't tell Deirdre; she'd kill me if she knew what a mess I had got myself into. Joe, Mixer, and Thom were not options either. I didn't want to face them anyway.

I texted Neil.

Let me make it clear: I was still upset with Neil. He had snapped my friend's skateboard in half, even if that friend had beat the fuck out of me. However, I needed someone's help to pull off what I needed to pull off.

I asked to meet Neil at the café we had met at before. He arrived before me and looked shaky-like, definitely nervous. He started talking before I even sat down.

"Bobby, I want to apologise. I had no right and I was out of my head. I saw what they had done to you and I..."

I waved my hands. "Don't worry about it." Neil lowered his brows. "Really?"

"Yeah. Don't do it again, like, but yeah." Neil exhaled and nodded.

"That's great, Bobby. I thought for sure I'd blown it."

"You haven't. Though I do need your help with something," I said.

Neil put his elbows on the table and leaned forward slightly.

"Anything. What is it?"

"I need you to help me put on a funeral." The server showed up at this moment.

"What can I get ya's?" she asked. Neil looked at me sideways before looking at her.

"Water's, um, fine for me, thanks," he said before looking back at me.

"Can I get a Coke?" I asked. I was feeling slightly fired up, I'll be honest.

The server walked away as Neil leaned forward again. He furrowed his brow deeper, looked off to the side, then at me.

"Who died?" he whispered.

"Nobody. Well, nobody real," I responded. Neil shook his head. "I'm lost."

"Jinky," I said.

Neil considered for a second before he seemed to remember.

"Fake Jinky, right?" he asked.

"Yes. Real Jinky died in 2006 of motor neurone disease."

"Jesus, Bobby. Why do you know that?" "Research."

"Why?" Neil asked. "Why what?"

"Why did you kill fake Jinky?"

"Well... it was impulsive, I'll be honest." Neil cocked his head.

"In any case," I started again. "I killed him. He's dead." The server arrived with the drinks.

"One water," she said, putting the water down in front of Neil. "And one Coke."

She put the Coke in front of me and I started drinking it quickly. I drank it too quickly, though, and started to cough.

"Wrong pipe," I choked out. Neil was shaking his head.

"Why did you kill the man you made up?" he said, almost to himself. "I don't understand."

"It's a long story," I responded. "I was mad... it doesn't matter. Now the lads on the forum want to come to the service. So we have to have a service."

Neil sat back in the seat.

"You realise how much work a funeral service requires, let alone money? You need a church involved; you need a grave plot. You need a body, Bobby."

I looked down at the table and nodded. I hadn't thought about the body.

"You're right," I whispered. "So are you gonna help me or not?"

Neil stuck his tongue into his bottom lip then sighed. "All right, mate. I'll help you."

We left the café and walked to a funeral parlour about ten minutes away. We stuck our heads in and there was an older man sitting down in the lobby, reading the newspaper.

Neil looked at me, then at him, and started talking. "Hiya, I'm Neil. This here is Bobby."

"Hello," the man said, looking up from his newspaper and nodding.

"We're not... interrupting anything, yeah? No... funerals today?"

"Aye, you're nae interrupting anything."

"Right, then," Neil nodded. "We have a, um... an interesting one for you. I'm sure you haven't heard about something like it before."

"Let's hear it."

"We want to bury someone. And honor this person, but we don't have... we don't have the body."

"Don't have the body?"

"No."

The man pursed his lips then shrugged. "How do you know they're dead, then?"

"We were there. Or at least I was. He was my brother, and he was sick. It was very peaceful. But he, um... always had a dream of... of donating his body to science, and the like."

"Ah," the man said, nodding. "I see."

"So, I guess," Neil continued after a moment of silence. "My question is, about the legality of burying... nothing."

The man closed his newspaper and looked up at the ceiling.

"You know, to be perfectly honest... I'm not really sure." "I'm sorry?"

"We've done it for soldiers and the like. Or nasty accidents. Closed caskets. I suppose we could... put nothing in there."

"But you don't know if that's... precisely legal, then?"

"Well, to make it whatever risk there may be, might cost ya something dear," the man said before opening his newspaper again.

Neil sighed. He walked over to a table in the corner of the room, where there were notecards with the parlour's name on the top. He grabbed a pen, put it to his lips, and wrote something down. He then walked over to the man and handed it to the man, who accepted it without looking.

"Jesus, mate," the man said. "For this, I'll jump in the box meself."

Neil took care of the details with the man, called Mr. Murphy.

"Saturday, then?" Neil asked. "Saturday," the man confirmed.

We walked out of the funeral parlour and Neil looked up at the sky.

"Fucking hell, I need a cigarette," he mumbled, reaching into his pocket.

"You all right?" I asked him.

"This funeral is gonna cost me a fortune, mate," Neil said, sticking a cigarette in his mouth.

"Well," I started. "If it means anything, I really appreciate it."

Neil looked at me before lighting his cigarette.

"Thanks, Bobby. Can I cash that? Gratitude?" Then he smiled at me.

"I'll deal with that shite, mate. You focus on school."

I nodded. "I should definitely focus on maths, since I failed that last exam especially."

Neil took the cigarette out of his mouth. "Since you what?"

MEMORIAL SERVICES FOR JINKY
Posted by JungleBhoy
hi all,
i first wanted to thank every single person who's reached
out to me about my father, Jinky. the kindness shown by
all of you is something I'll never forget
we're having services for Jinky on Saturday, starting at
noon at Murphy's Funeral Parlour (address below)
thank you again, and hope to see you there

Chapter Twenty-Three

My nose was feeling better. It didn't hurt like shite to touch anymore, so that seemed an improvement.

I did as Neil asked and focused on schoolwork. I revised for a Physics exam that I'm very confident I failed.

Luckily, for my maths exam that I failed, teacher let me correct my answers for half points back.

But yeah, probably still failed my Physics exam.

I texted Neil and asked him if he needed any help with the funeral.

"eulogy?" he texted back.

I like writing, so this sounded nice. But when I sat down to write out what I would say about Jinky, I couldn't come up with anything beyond "nice" and "good." Deirdre was in the TV room, so I went to her and brought my notebook and pencil.

"Young Bob," she said, wearing her reading glasses. "How ya doing?"

"Good, Deirdre. I have homework, though, and was wondering if you might be able to help?" "Is it maths?" "No."

"Then I'm free as a bird," Deirdre said, earmarking her page in her book. "What's the assignment?"

"I need to write a eulogy–" I said, sitting down on the couch next to her.

"Who for?"

"Well, anyone we want, really." Deirdre cocked her head.

"Seems an odd assignment. What's the point of it?" "Not sure. Anyway, yeah, I thought I'd…" I trailed off. I didn't know if I wanted to finish my sentence. But I did. "What do you remember most about my mum?" Deirdre's eyebrows raised quickly before she took her reading glasses off.

"Oh. Well," she started. "I think it's more important what you remember, Bob."

I put my pencil to my mouth. "She was kind."

"Mhmm. What else?"

"Smart. Even with maths and sciences and stuff." "What else?" Deirdre asked, putting her glasses on the couch between us.

"She was warm," I said. "She was warm and... she always knew what to say. To make me feel better." Deirdre swallowed. I could see tears in her eyes, I think. "What else?"

"She had a strange laugh," I said, laughing myself. Deirdre let out a laugh that turned more into a cry. "It was low even though her voice wasn't."

I saw a tear fall down Deirdre's cheek.

"What else?"

I thought for a second.

"We would dance," I said, sniffling now. "We were both shite at it but we would dance whenever a song she liked came on the radio."

Deirdre took my hand.

"She was the best," I said, tears falling off my face now. Deirdre nodded and squeezed my hand.

"She was."

I still hated lying to Deirdre, even if she was something of a sleuth who was often able to find out things I'd hidden. She had found out I was spending time with Neil, after all.

It's not that Deirdre *can't* know; maybe I could explain it all to her. But it seems late in the game to tell her.

I vow to never lie to Deirdre again, as long as I live. Starting after the funeral.

Chapter Twenty-Four

It's Saturday. Funeral day.

I wore my best outfit – a shirt and jeans – and showed up to the funeral parlour. Neil was outside, dressed in his usual nicely-tailored suit.

"Christ, Bobby," he said, throwing up his hands. "Jeans again?"

"It's all I've got," I responded.

"Should've gotten you a suit for this. Here, put this on," he said, taking off his coat and holding it out for me. I put my arms through it and he slid it up my shoulders. "It'll be tight but will look... better, I suppose."

"Thanks, Neil." Neil nodded.

"Right, then. Ready?" I nodded back.

All we had to do was get through those next few hours.

The first few people showed up around 12:05pm. They introduced themselves as lads from the forum. I remember one of them was 6er but can't remember the other one. I had to explain that Jinky was not one for pictures, which is why there were absolutely none of him in the building. "He would've hated that," I said a lot.

Then more lads showed up. Then a few more.

Then Fred, Geoff, and Sam arrived. They wrapped me in some kind of a group hug. It was quite nice.

"We're sorry, mate," Fred said. "Jinky was a legend." "Absolute legend," Geoff confirmed.

"We're here for you, mate. Whatever you need," Sam said, putting his hand on the back of my head.

Mr. Murphy led me and Neil to the side of the casket, and a line formed. People walked up to the casket.

Some put their hands on it. A few kneeled in front of it on the kneeler. Then they shook our hands and told us how sorry they were for our loss. I assured them I'd be fine. I genuinely tried to convey that it would be okay, but everyone still looked so sorry.

People began to sit in the seats in front of the casket. Then all the eyes seemed to shift to me. I was still standing next to the casket. They were seemingly waiting for me to say something. There wouldn't be a church service. We wouldn't be going to a cemetery.

I stepped in front of the casket. I reached into my jeans pocket and pulled out the piece of paper I wrote the eulogy on. My hands were shaking as I started reading.

"Thank you all for coming. Really. It means a lot to me and... my uncle," I said, turning to Neil. I turned back and cleared my throat. "Jinky was..."

I couldn't speak. My throat was dry. I felt sweat in my armpits. I couldn't speak at all.

"Jinky was, uh..."

I saw eyes move to the floor. No one wanted to look at this.

"Jinky was love," Neil said. He nodded to me. I nodded back. He stepped towards me. He stood next to me. "He was a beam of pure light. He was good. Just *good*. And he had so much love in his heart that he couldn't possibly give all of away if he tried."

Neil looked at me. I was starting to cry again. Christ, I've been crying a lot lately.

"And he tried, his absolute hardest, to give out as much love as he could. Even to people... who didn't deserve it. We lost touch for a while... me and Jinky. I thought about... I regret everyday not reaching out before it was..."

I heard Neil sniffle. At least I wasn't alone.

"But he lives on. Through the most important person in the world to me. Through Bobby. And I'm thankful every day that I have the opportunity to be his... uncle," Neil said, and put his hand on my shoulder. He gripped it.

And I knew who he was actually talking about.

People started to file out a little later on. Neil and I sort of avoided eye contact, it felt like.

I did have a question for him. "Did you mean it?"

Neil then looked at me. He didn't break eye contact. "I meant it."

Chapter Twenty-Five

I felt great for the week after the funeral.

Often in football, when a new manager comes in and takes charge, a lot is made about "a new era" or some such.

Well, the Jinky Era is over. The JungleBhoy Era has begun.

And I didn't fail my Physics exam!

It was Saturday today, and I was in my bed when I heard the front door open. I heard chatting in the hall before there was a knock on my door.

"Yeah?" I shouted.

"You decent?" Deirdre shouted back through the door. "Yes, Deirdre."

"You sure?"

"Yes, just come in!" I shouted back.

Deirdre opened the door; Neil was standing next to her. His overcoat was buttoned all the way up.

I got up on my hands, still under the blankets. Neil nodded at me.

"All right, Bobby," he said. "All right, Neil," I said back.

Deirdre winked at me. "I'll leave you to it," she said, leaving the door open and walking down the hall. Neil turned as she walked away.

"Thank you, Dee."

His hands were in his coat pocket.

"May I come in?" he asked. I nodded again.

"So, how does it feel now that the whole ordeal is over?" he asked in almost a whisper.

"Keep your voice down, Neil," I whispered back. "I said it quiet, mate."

"I feel good, actually. I feel like Jinky made, I don't know… made people feel good in some kind of way," I said.

"Well, what I feel, mate – and what I've felt since I finally got to spend some time with you – is absolute pride in who my son is. And shame for not having been there for him all his life."

I didn't expect that. Not at all. He nodded quickly.

"That's changing. All right? You're stuck with me, mate, sorry to say," Neil said.

I nodded and stuck my hand out. "Right, then," I said, smiling.

"Right, then," he smiled back, and shook my hand. He inhaled sharply and rose to his feet.

"Now get ready or we'll be late," he said. "Late for what?" I laughed.

He pulled out a folded Celtic scarf and unfurled it, then wrapped it around his neck.

"Come on, then. Or I'll have to go with your Auntie Dee," he continued, smiling.

My eyes opened wide. "You're joking," I whispered.

"Fine. Have it your way," he answered, looking at his watch. "I'll go ask her if she wants your ticket."

I sprang from my bed and went to my closet. I rifled through school shirts and dress shirts and found my Celtic jumper. I threw it on as fast as I could as Neil left the room and headed toward the front door. Running out of the room, I nearly bowled over Deirdre, who wrapped a Celtic scarf around my neck.

"Your mum's," she whispered in my ear before she kissed me on the cheek. I knew it was mum's, but I hadn't seen it in a while.

"Come on then, mate." Neil gestured at me with his head.

"Have fun!" Deirdre shouted after me.

"Thank you, Deirdre!" I shouted back. I saw Neil smile in Deirdre's direction before he closed the door behind me.

It's a cliché, but the atmosphere at Celtic Park was electric. Even on the train, everyone was buzzing. I don't think Neil and I said a word the entire trip. I also don't think I'd smiled harder or for longer in my entire life.

I hadn't been to a match at Celtic Park since my mum died. I used to go with her, and it felt odd to go without her. But this, going with Neil... I'm not sure how she'd feel about it. But I knew I was ready for it.

We got to our seats and I looked around me. I used my eyes the way a director would use a camera: I panned side-to-side; I tilted my head up and down; I tried to record it in my head from every angle I possibly could.

I looked over to Neil, who was smiling. He looked at me and nodded.

I nodded back.

More projects
coming from

cosmorama

www.cosmoramaofficial.com

H.M. Ryan is a writer from the Philadelphia area. He has written over fifteen hundred novels, all of them very long and well-respected and studied in schools for being good.

He is not married but would like to be at some point, he thinks.